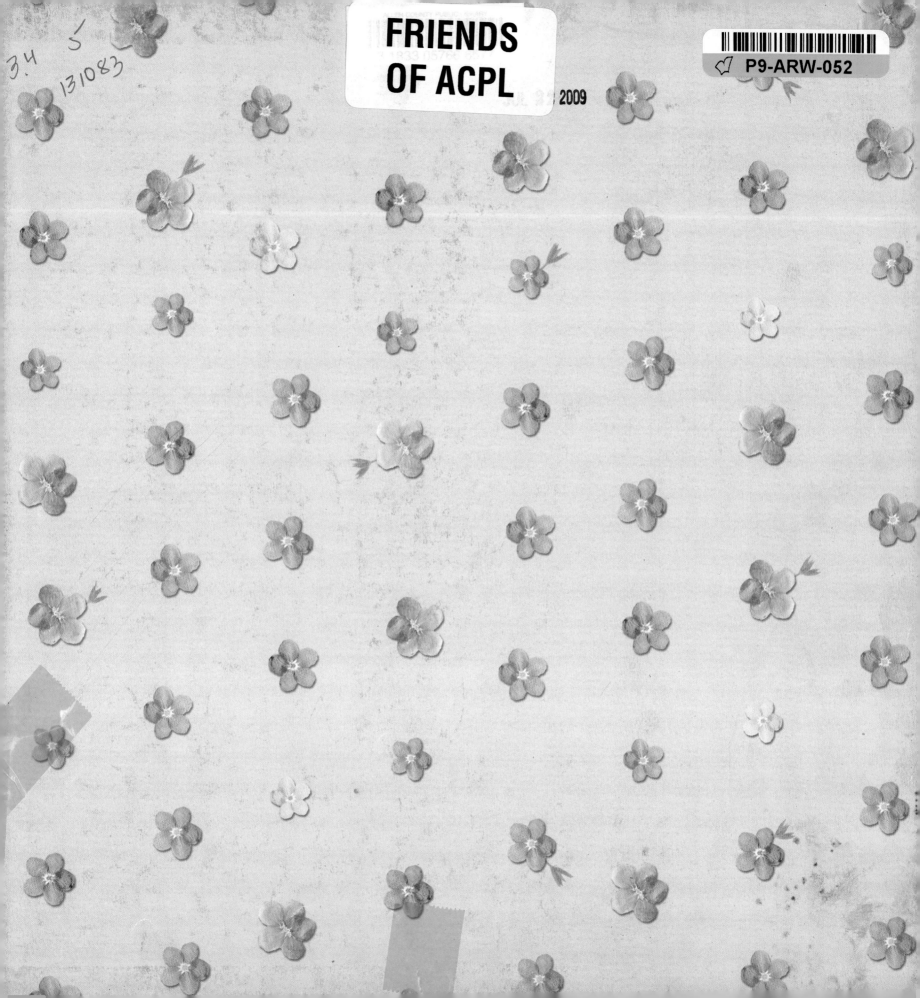

For my sister, Jackie - who taught me how to draw kites.

First edition for the United States and Canada
published in 2009 by Barron's Educational Series, Inc.

First published in 2009 by Hodder Children's Books

ISBN-13: 978-0-7641-6200-8
ISBN-10: 0-7641-6200-4

Library of Congress Control Number: 2008931750

All inquiries should be addressed to:
Barron's Educational Series, Inc.
250 Wireless Blvd.
Hauppauge, New York 11788
www.barronseduc.com

Printed in China
9 8 7 6 5 4 3 2 1

Can you spot the dung beetles?

Forget*Me*Not

Michael Broad

BARRON'S

As the herd crossed the plains, one little elephant was tired of walking.

"Mama, I'm bored," sighed Monty, dragging his trunk along the dusty ground.

"The rain is coming soon," said his mother.
"Then there'll be forget-me-nots."

"What are forget-me-nots?"
asked Monty.

"Tiny blue flowers," replied his mother,
"to help elephants remember."

"Remember what, Mama?" he asked.

"Remember to stay with the herd,"
she warned.

"Oh, I won't forget that," said Monty confidently. "What else?"

"Never forget how much I love you," she smiled.

Later, Monty saw something strange beside a tree and, forgetting his mother's warning, he stopped to investigate.

The little elephant sniffed and prodded and plucked the blue thing right out of the ground.

"A forget-me-not!" he gasped excitedly. "I will take it straight to Mama."

But when Monty looked around...

the herd was nowhere to be seen.

A flock of flamingos was gathered nearby, so the little elephant hurried over. "I found a forget-me-not, but forgot something important!" said Monty.

"You forgot to stay with the flock!" shrieked the flamingos.

"I don't think I belong to a flock," Monty frowned.

"But the rain is coming!" they squawked.

"How will you find SHELTER without a flock to huddle with?"

"I don't remember," sighed Monty.

The young elephant kept walking until he came upon a mob of meerkats. "I found a forget-me-not, but forgot something important!" said Monty.

"You forgot to stay with the mob!"

chuckled the meerkats.

"I don't think I belong to a mob," Monty frowned.

"But the rain
is coming!"
they added.
"How will you
play without
a mob to LOOK
OUT for you?"

"I don't
remember,"
sighed Monty.

As the sun began to set, the little elephant discovered
a colony of termites. "I found a forget-me-not,
but forgot something important!" said Monty.

"You forgot
to stay with
the colony!"
gasped the termites.

"I don't think I belong to a colony,"
Monty frowned.

"But the rain is coming!"
they said.
"How will you build
a HOME without a colony?"

Monty couldn't remember, and shed a tear on the dusty ground. This was followed by another, and another, until there were too many tears to count.

The little elephant looked up and saw they were not teardrops at all, but raindrops.

"The rain **HAS COME!**"

yelled the termites, and they disappeared inside their mounds.

Monty was all alone as the rain came down,
but as the drops of water plopped into the broken
bucket he recalled his mother's words.

"Never forget how much I love you," she had said.

And Monty remembered
how Mama SHELTERED him.

And how she always
LOOKED OUT for him.

And how the herd was his HOME.

Holding the memory close
to his heart, the brave little
elephant continued walking.

But it rained so hard that Monty could not see where he was going. BUMP! He walked straight into a small group of trees.

"Shelter," Monty thought, and hid beneath them.
"I'll wait here till the rain stops."

He thought he heard someone call his name, but it must have been the wind whistling through the leaves above.

Then he heard it again. "Monty!"

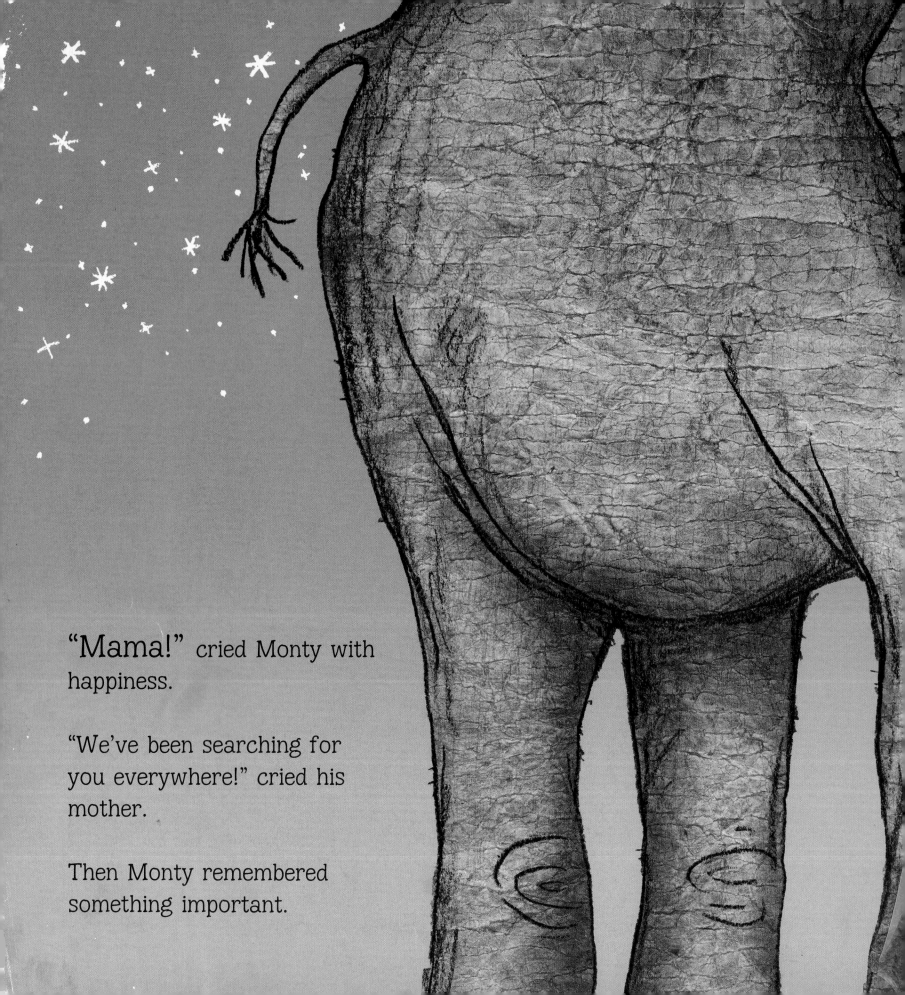

"Mama!" cried Monty with happiness.

"We've been searching for you everywhere!" cried his mother.

Then Monty remembered something important.

"I brought you a
forget-me-not, Mama,"
he yawned.

His mother took the
broken bucket and
placed it on her head.

"Thank you, Monty,"
she smiled. "It's the prettiest
forget-me-not I've ever seen."

When Monty woke up the next day, the plains were filled with tiny blue flowers! The little elephant strolled around, munching on the delicious forget-me-nots that help elephants remember.

And from that day on, Monty never forgot to stay with the herd,
or how much his Mama loved him.

And forever after, he was always called Forget*Me*Not.